BOY, WAS I MAD!

words by
Kathryn Hitte

pictures by
Mercer Mayer

Parents' Magazine Press · New York

*

to Barbara and Mort and their family

I was mad one day.
I mean I was REALLY mad!
So I ran away.

I stuck a sandwich in my pocket,
and I left my house fast,
and I didn't look back.
I wouldn't look back at that house for anything,
I was so mad that day —
that day when I ran away.

I turned the corner, and there was
a crane, hanging out over the street.
And a steam shovel was way down
in a big old hole about a block wide.
The shovel was grabbing up dirt
like they do, and men were digging
and men were pounding and climbing
and driving things.
There was clanging and banging
and scuttle and shouting,
and earth and cement and stuff.
And that crane went up, and up,
and UP.

I'd like to work a thing like that. I think some day
I will. "Boy!" I said. "Hey, look at that!" I said.
And one of the workmen grinned and gave me
a helmet to wear. Just like his.

It was great at that place.
It was so great I almost forgot how mad I was.
But then I remembered and went on my way.

Down the street I met a junk wagon.
I knew that horse and wagon.
The junk man gave me a ride—he often does that.
He even let me hold the reins and drive.
"Not many city boys know how to drive a horse,"
the junk man said.
"Nope, there's not many boys around here like you."

"I might have a horse of my own some day," I said.
"I think some day I will."

It was fun on that wagon, driving around.
Then I remembered how mad I was, so I climbed down.

A baby stopped crying when I came along.
She was funny and fat and I said, "Hi!"
And I made her laugh.
I saw a dog that was after a cat,
and I watched them go—*Wow*!

Then I stopped to pet another dog, and three more
old hounds came running up to me.
They all began to follow me up the street.

"Look," I said. "Look, you dogs. I can't play with you now.
I'm running away, see? So let me alone.
Go on, go back where you came from! Go home!"

But they still tagged along.
There isn't a dog that doesn't like *me*.
I might raise dogs for a living some day.
I think some day I will.

Well, then there was a crack in the sidewalk
where I saw a lot of ants.
There must have been about a hundred million ants,
and maybe more than that.

They were marching in a long single line
like Indians,
and climbing in and out of their anthills.
Some of them were really working, too—
pulling on a big dead bug.
I watched them for quite a while.
Ants are almost the best thing there is to watch.
I almost wished I wasn't so mad.
I could have stayed there
and watched those ants all day.

"Hi, Ted!"
(That's me.)
"Hey—hi, Tom!"
(Tom is a kid I know.)
Tom and his dad and his grandpa were
waiting at a bus stop for a bus.
"We're going uptown to the park," Tom said.
"Come along with us, Ted!"

Well—I was getting tired of walking,
and it was a pretty warm day.
It sure would be fun to run and talk
and horse around in the park with Tom.
I was mad all right, but—
"Sure, I'll go," I said. "Okay!"

We got to the park, and the grown-ups sat down
on a bench to talk.
But Tom and I did some stunts and things
like standing on our heads.

And I jumped farther than Tom,
and we climbed around on some big rocks.
And we wondered how it is that birds know how to fly.
We had a real great day.

When we came home, there was a kind of
pale white half-moon in the sky.
That was funny because it was still daylight.
I never saw the moon in the daytime before.

"I bet I go to the moon some day," I said.
"I bet some day I do.
Yes, sir, I'm going to get to that old moon.
You wait and see!"

Then just as I got in my house—
"Pete's sake!" I thought. "I FORGOT!
Here I am, HOME, instead of running away!
What should I do?"

Well—supper was on, and something
smelled good—Boy, did I eat!
And it was a real funny thing,
but I just wasn't mad anymore.

Mom smiled when I told her about it —
about all I'd done instead of running away.
And she said, "Oh, Teddy, I'm glad!
I'm glad you forgot and came on back home."
"So am I," I said. "Me, too, Mom."
And she didn't have to tell me to get ready for bed.
It sure felt good, that bed! I was really tired.
That was some day — that day when I ran away.